Come

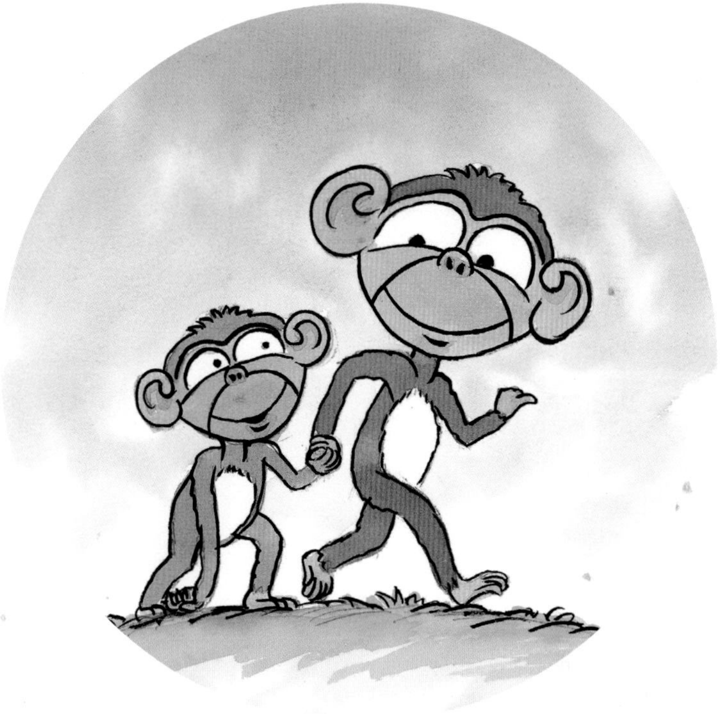

Illustrated by Dave Gunson

Rigby

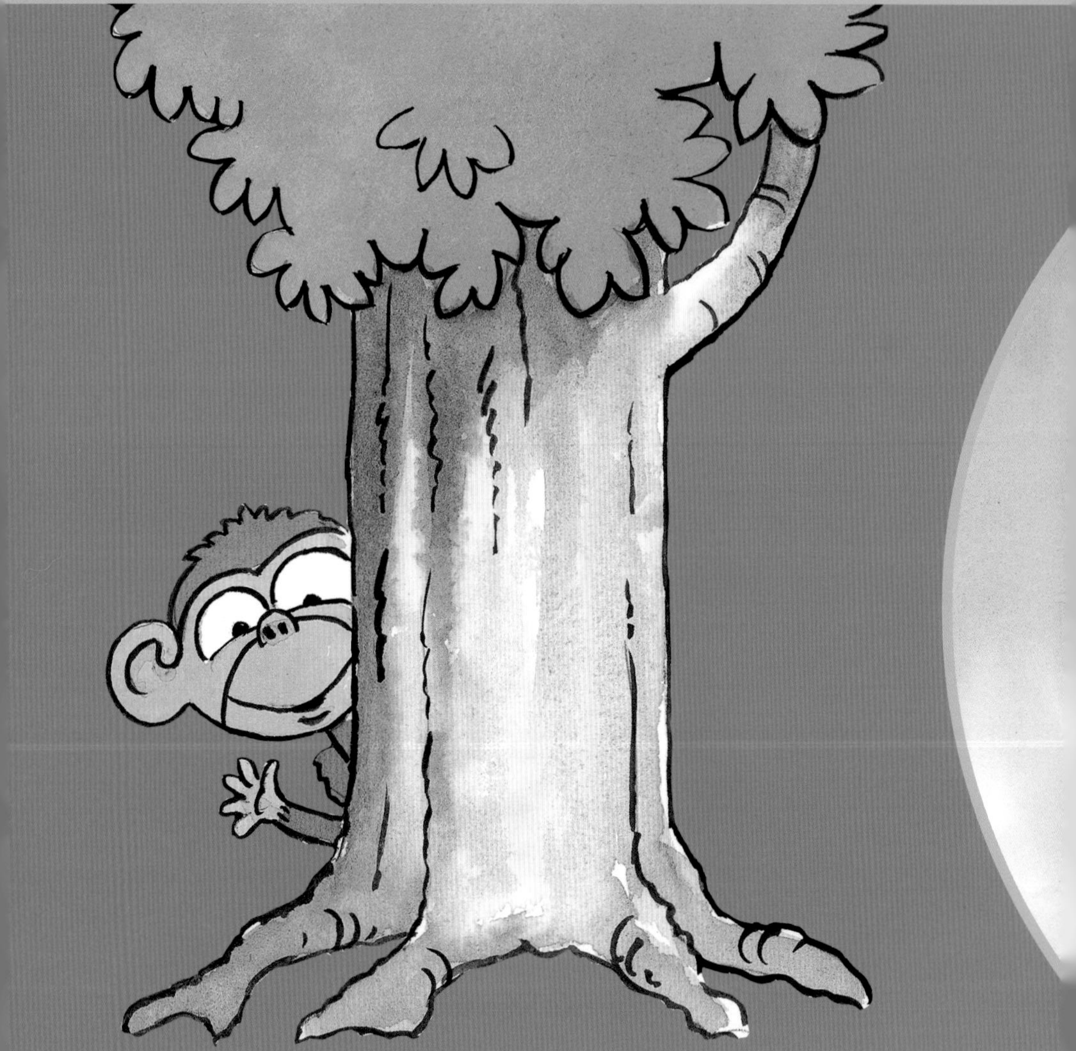

Come to the tree.

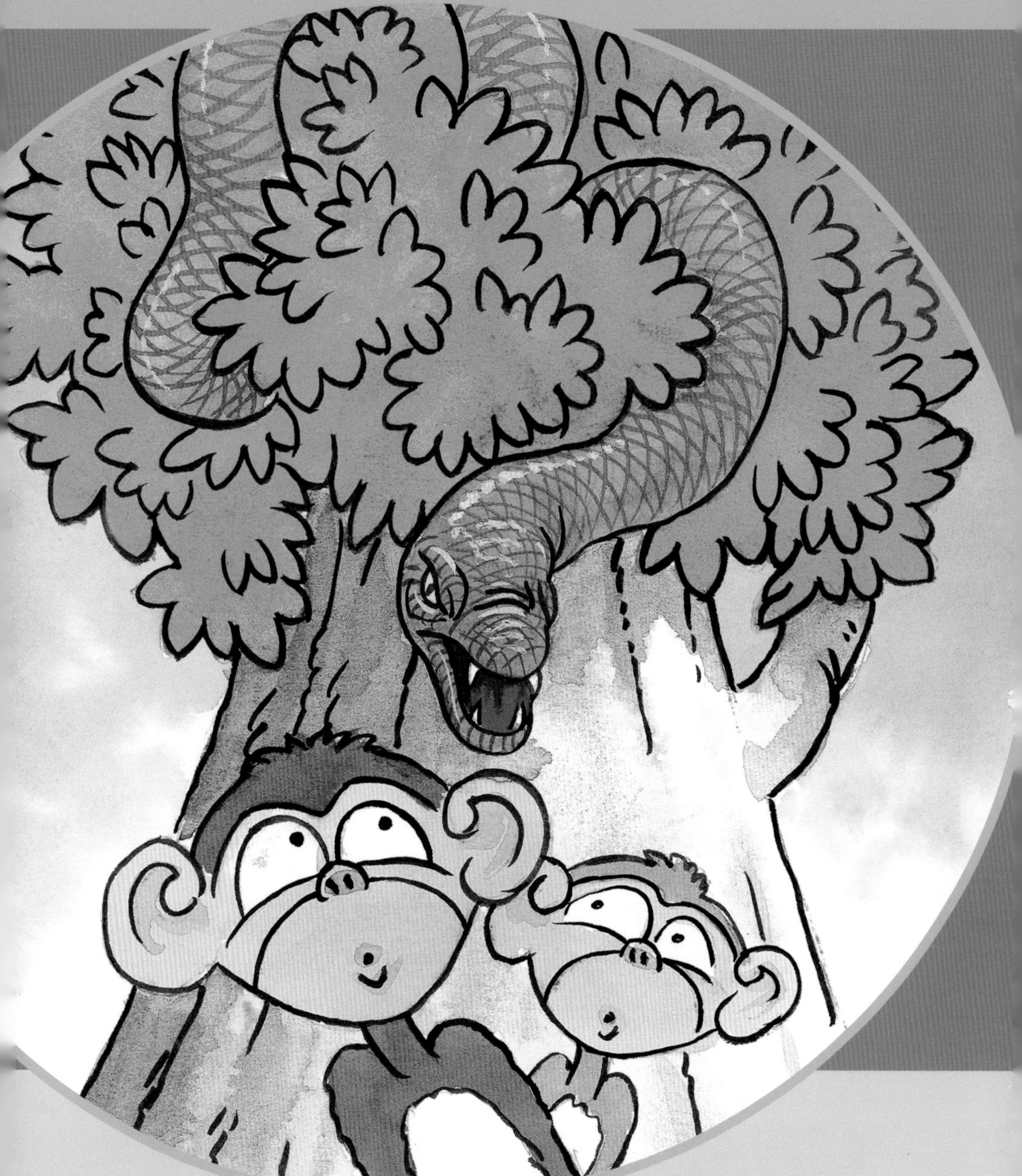

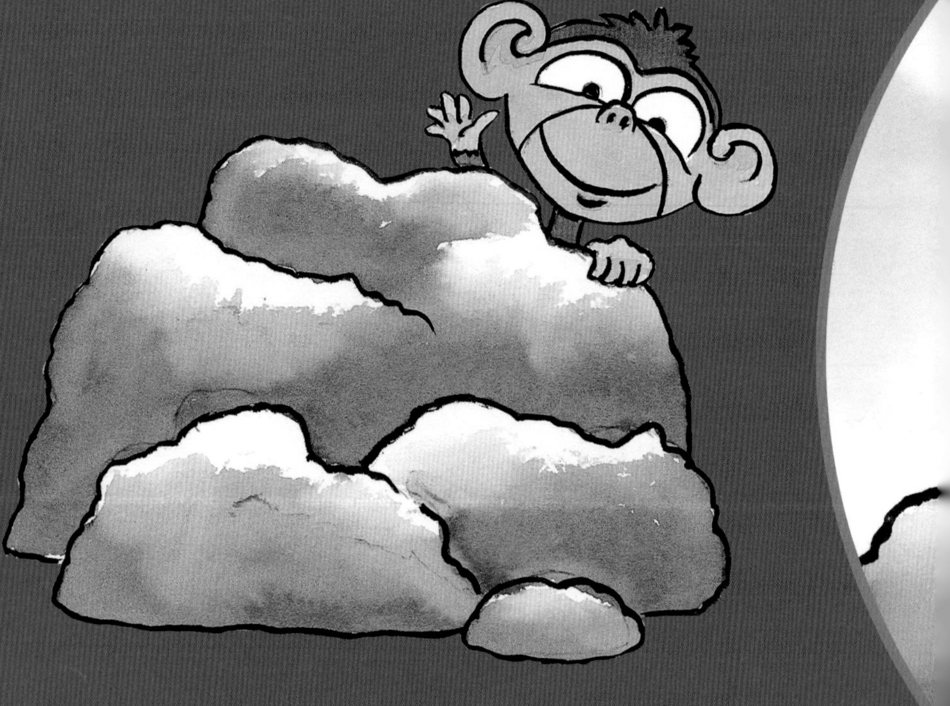

Come to the rock.

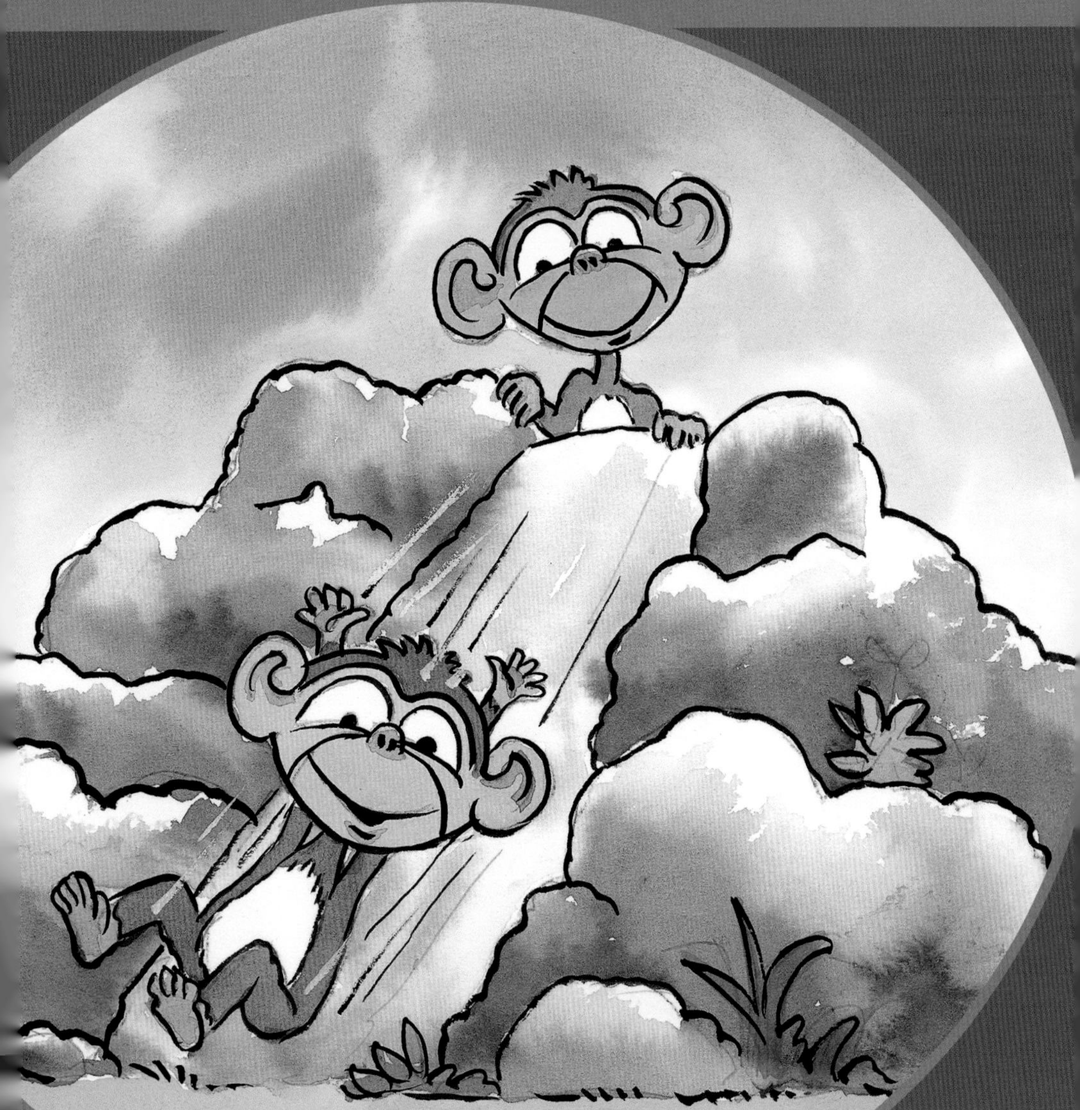

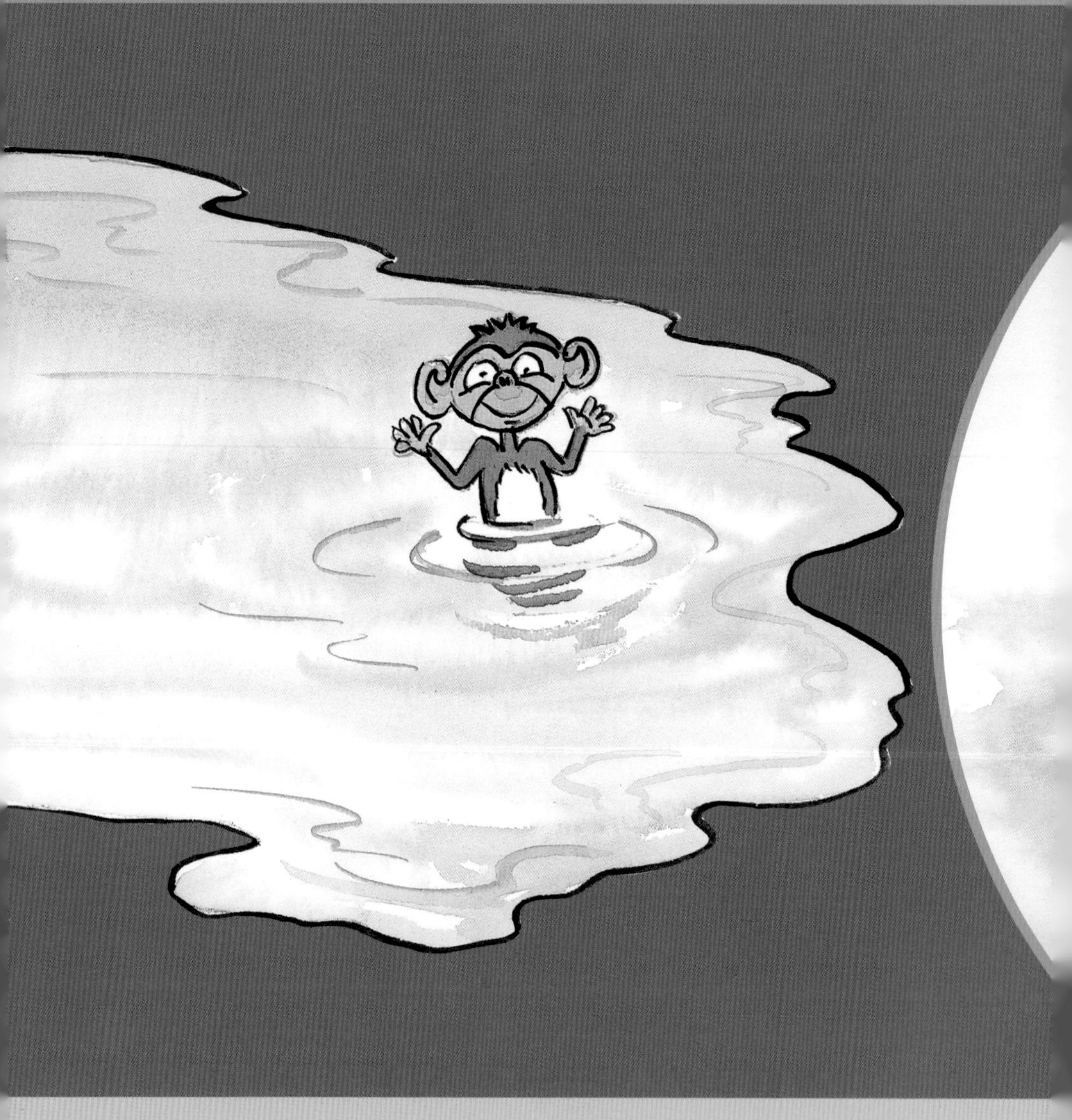

Come to the water.

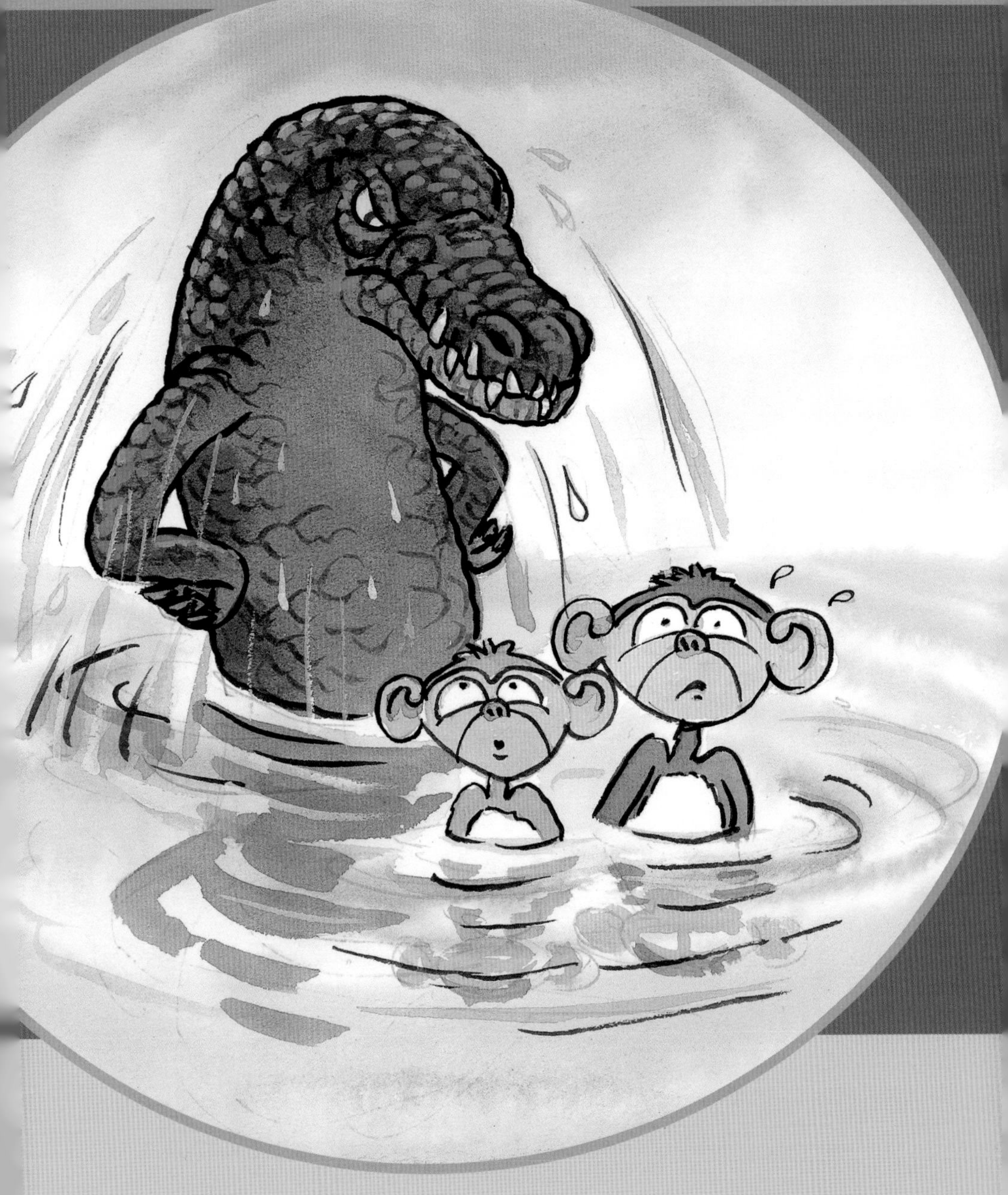

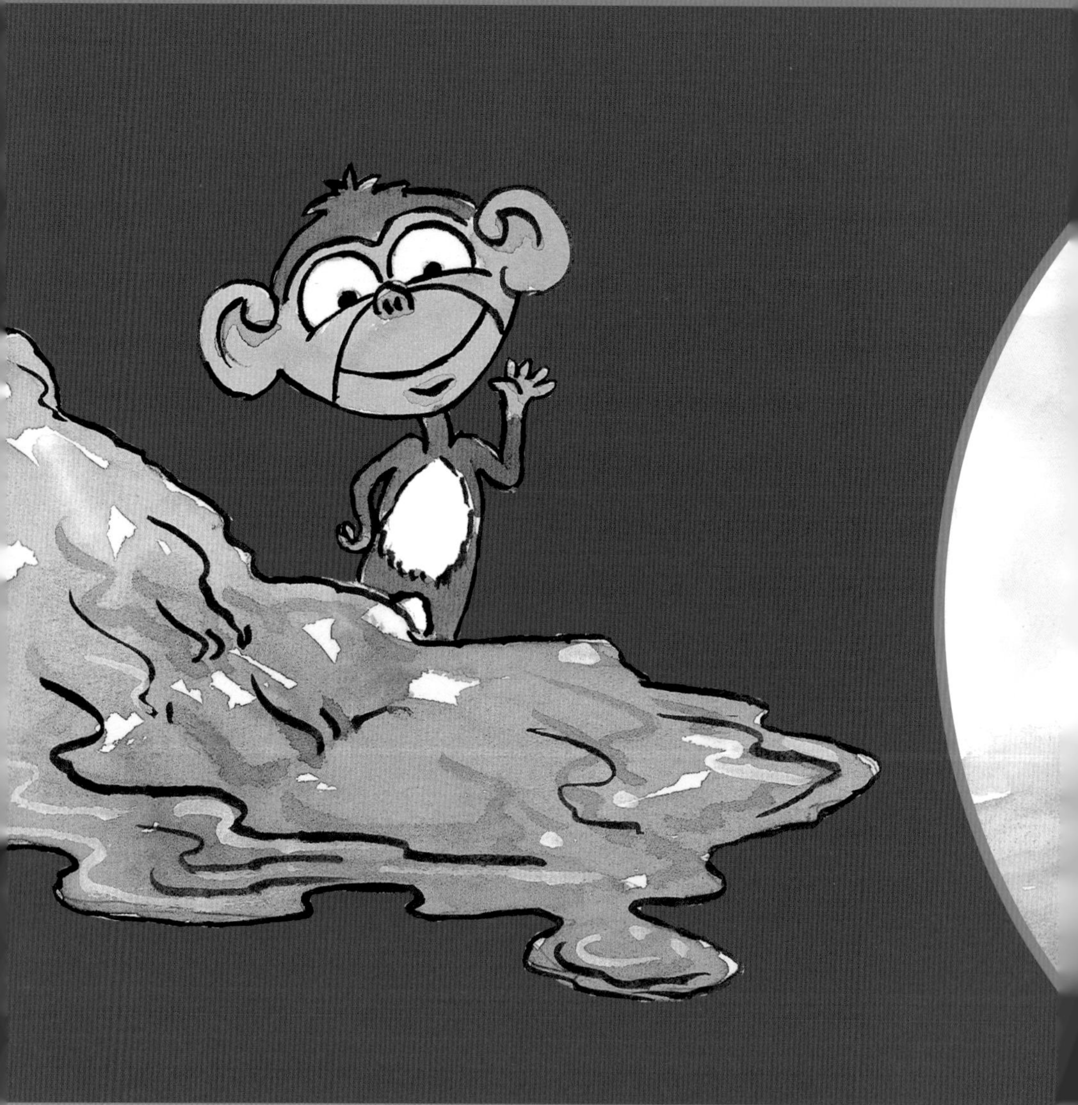

Come to the mud.

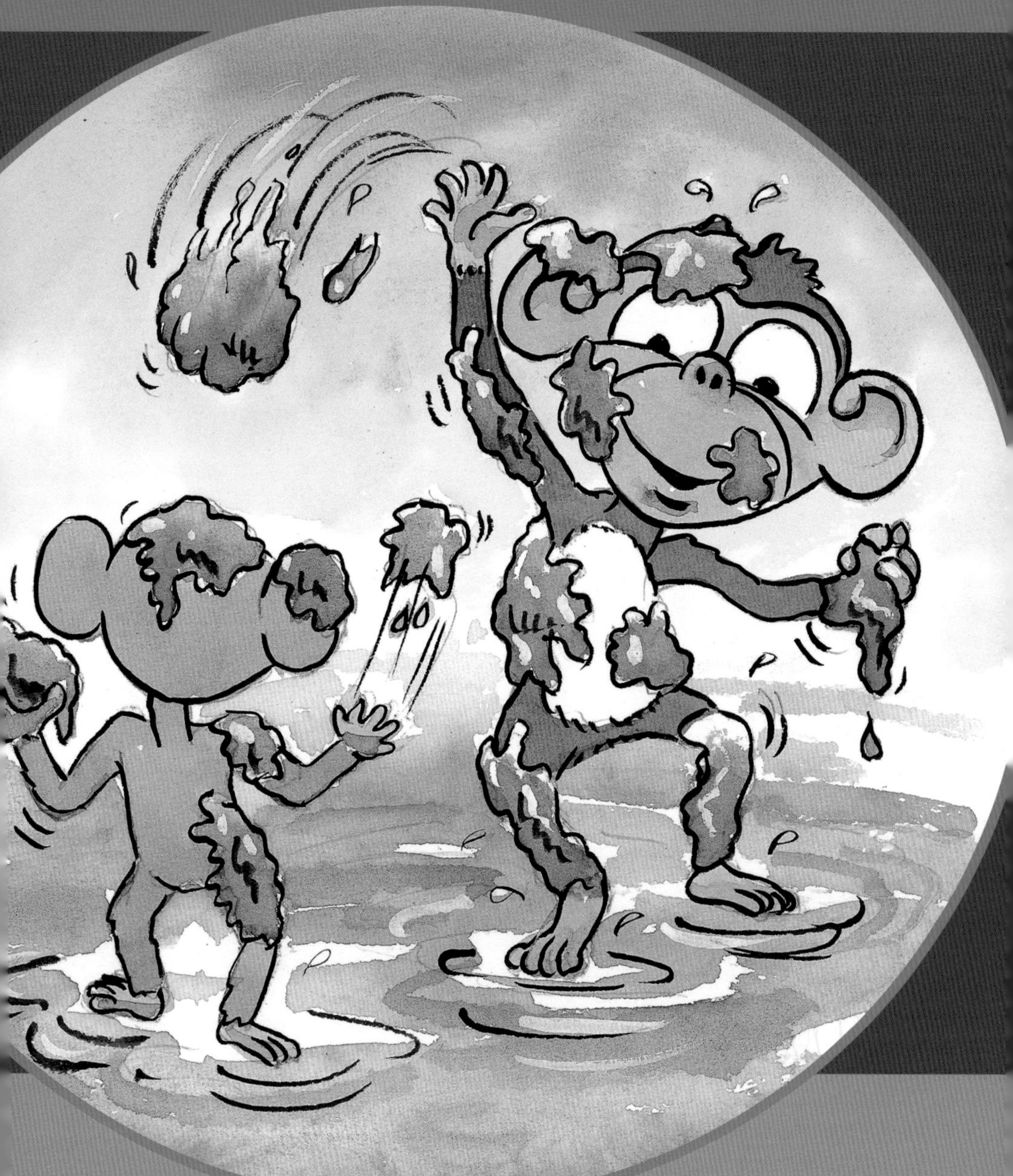

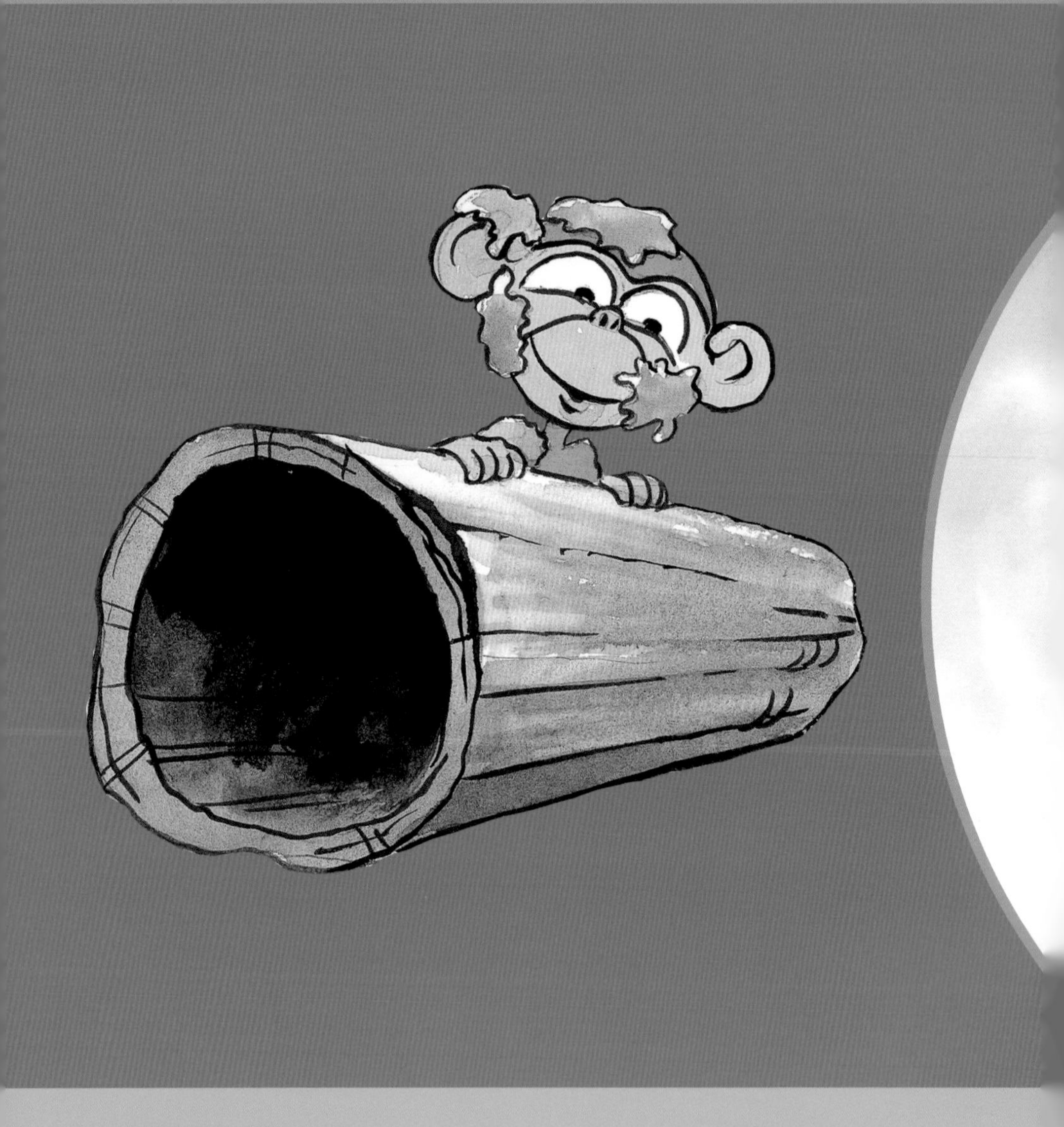

Come to the hole.

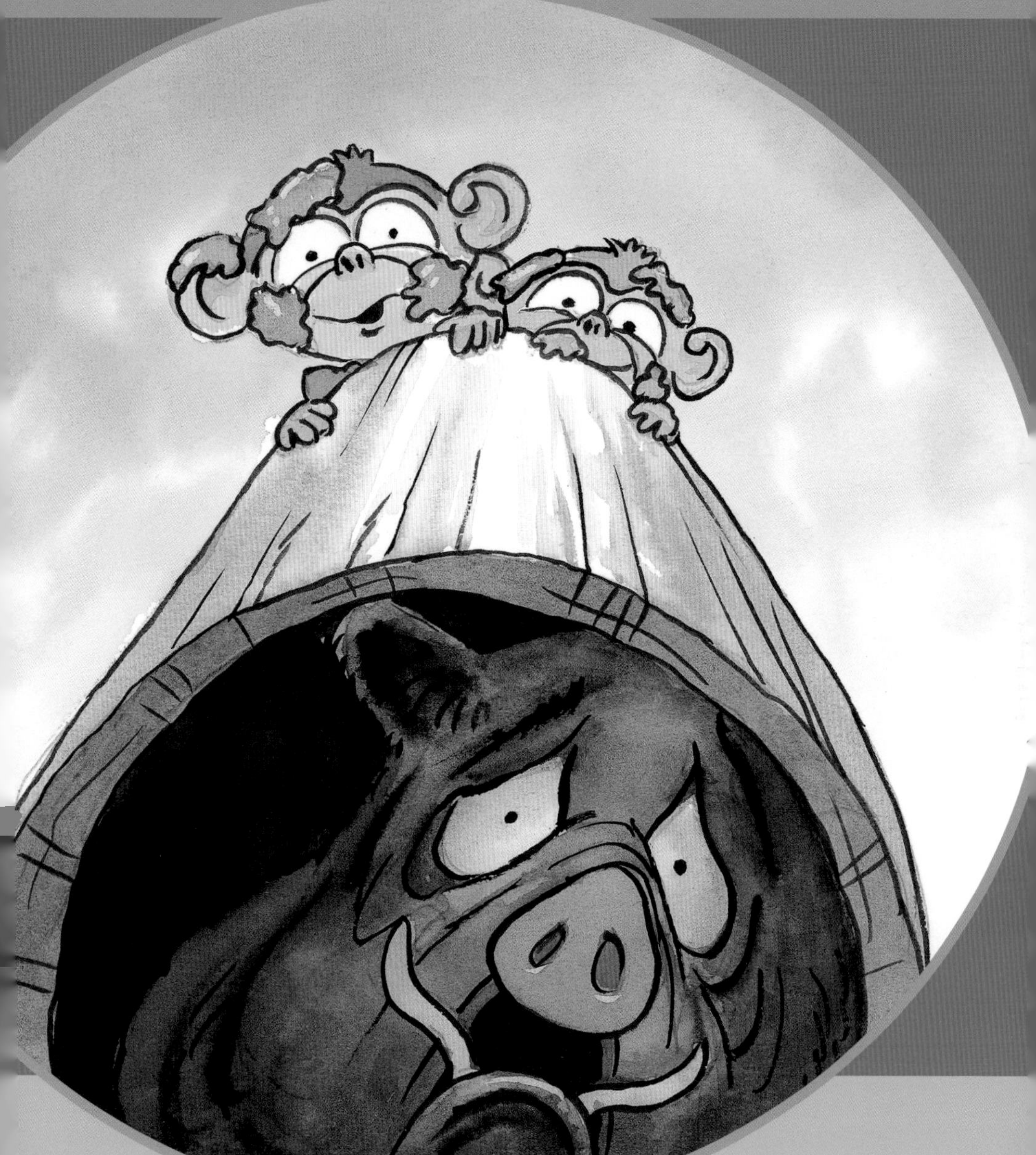

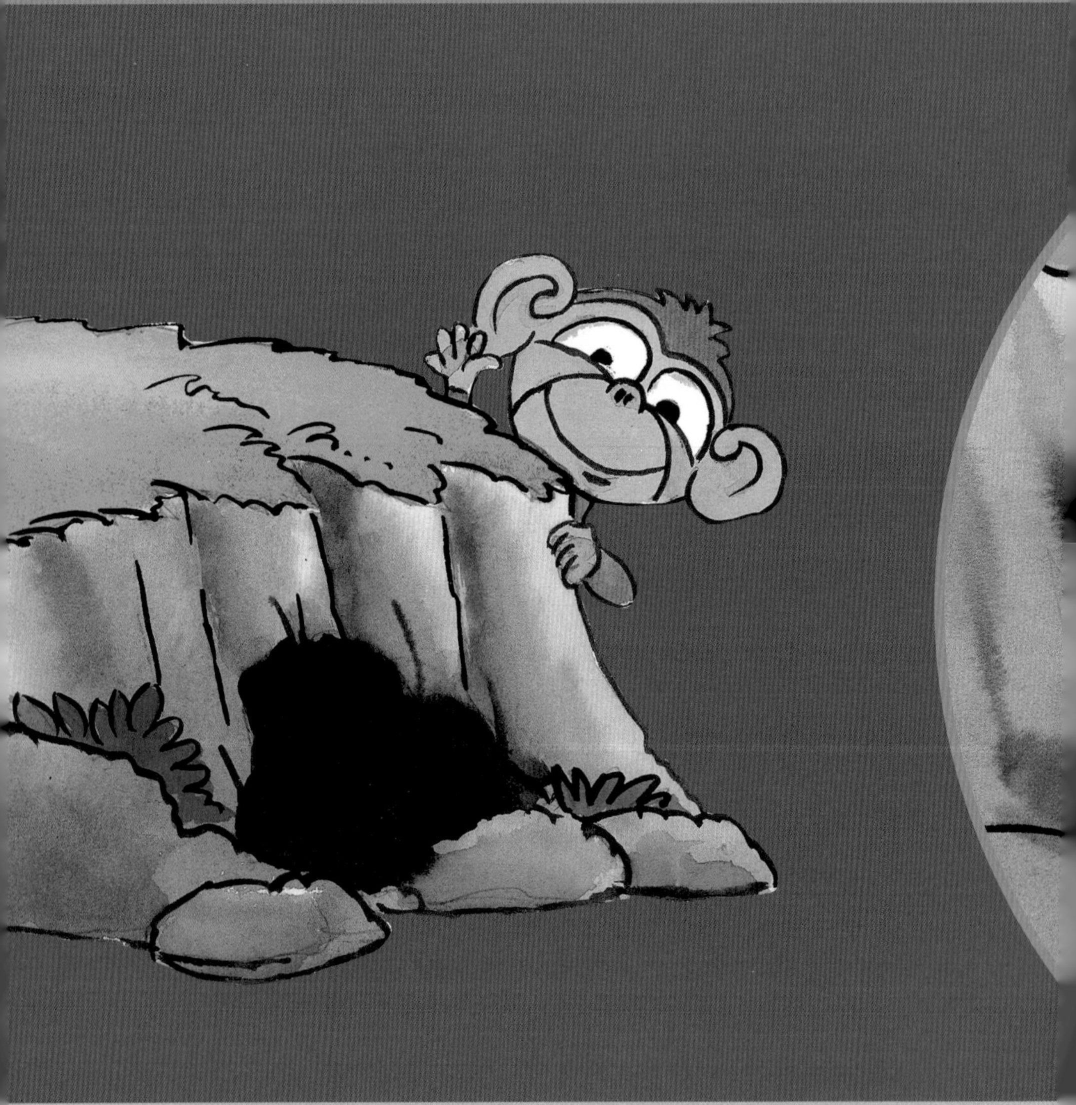

Come to the cave.

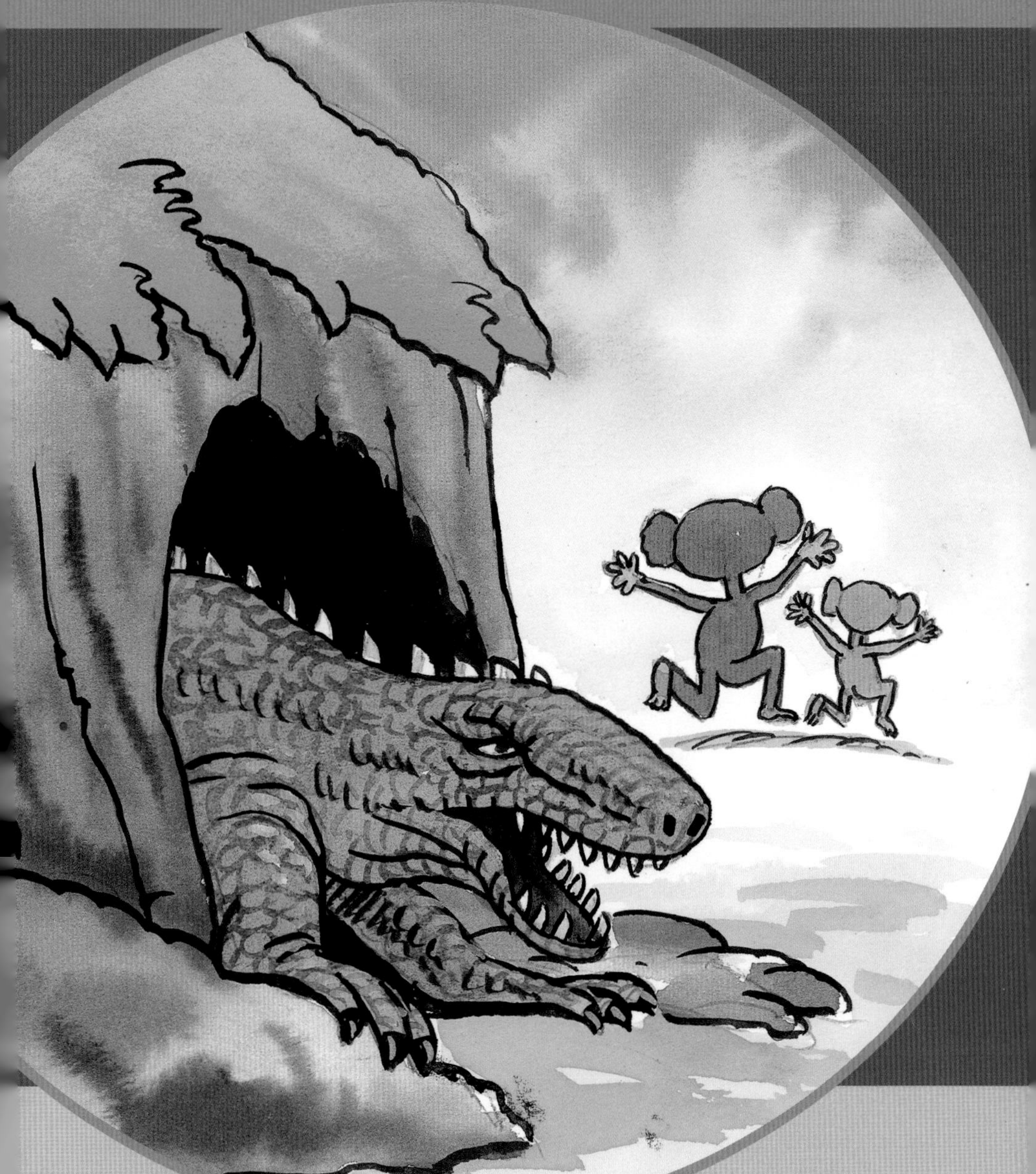

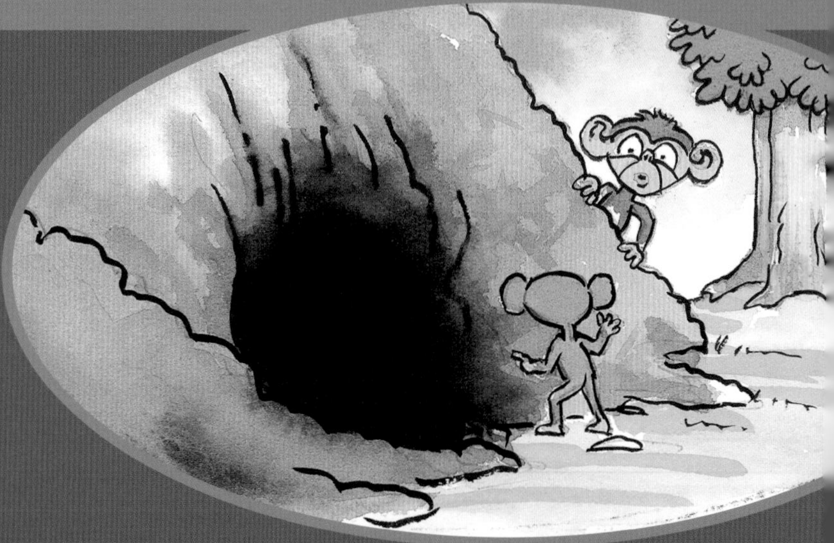

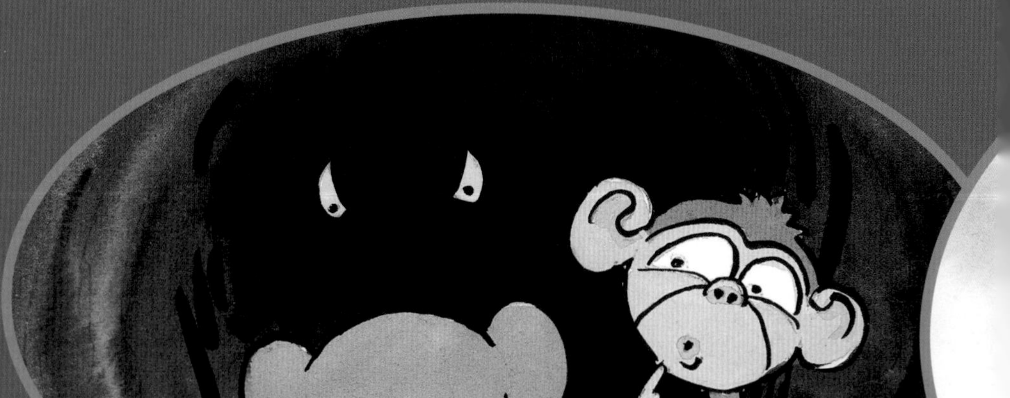

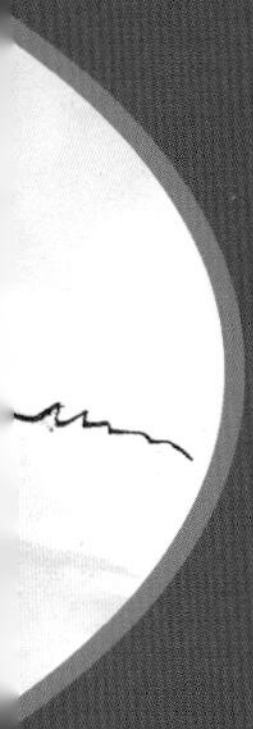

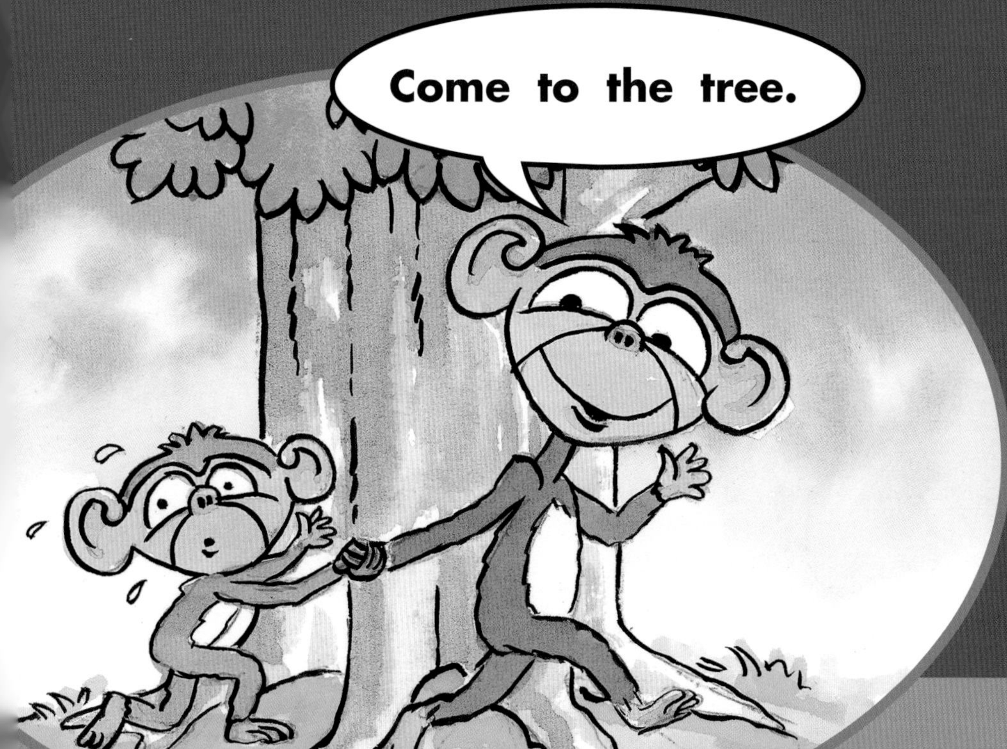
Come to the tree.

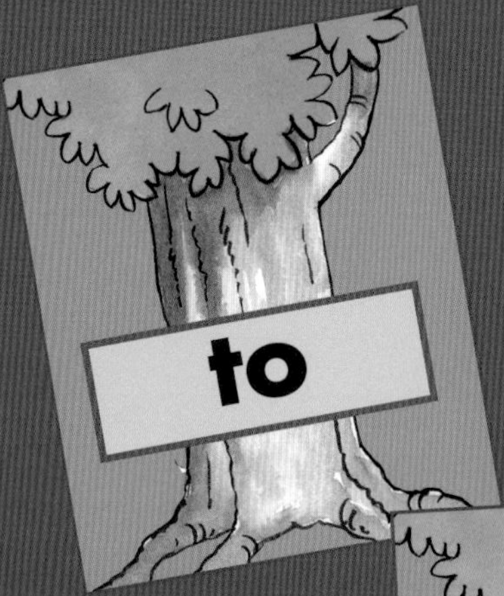
to
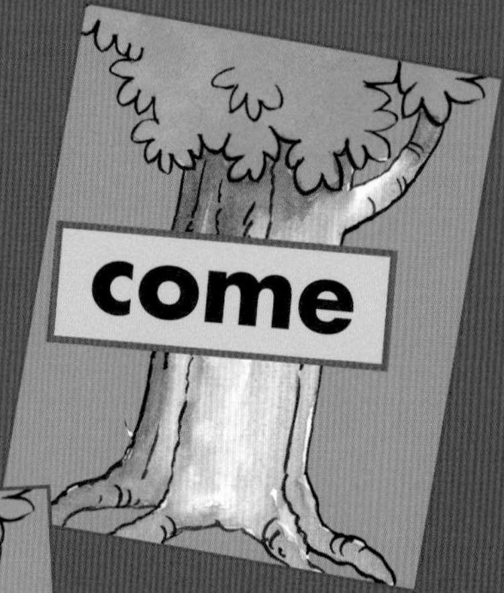
come
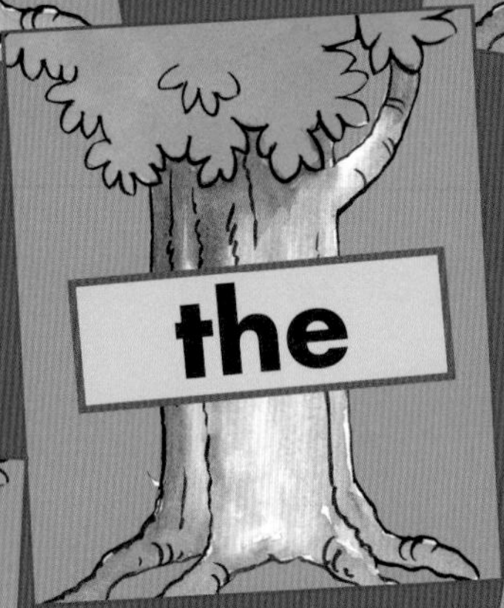
the
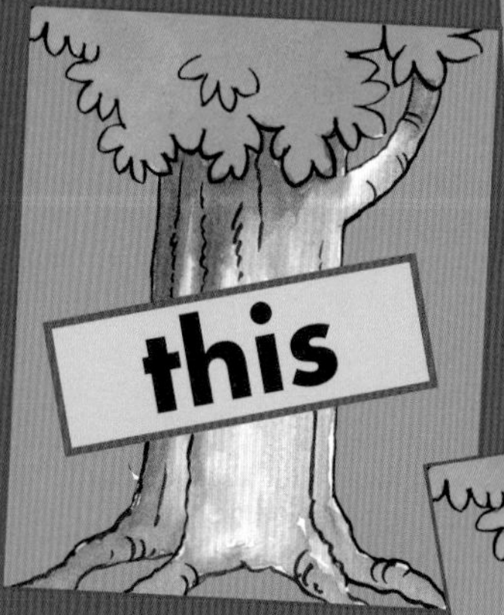
this
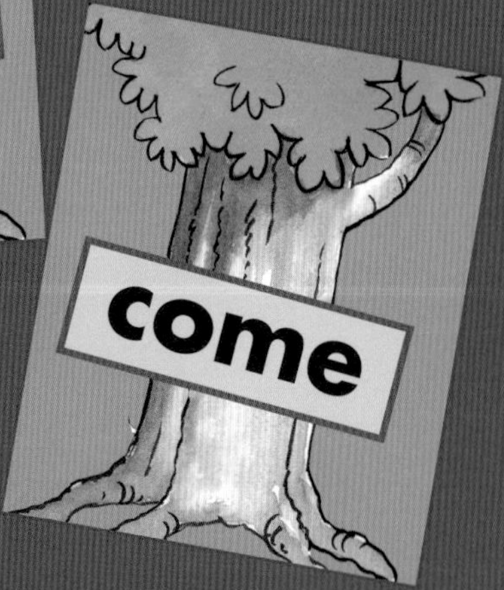
come
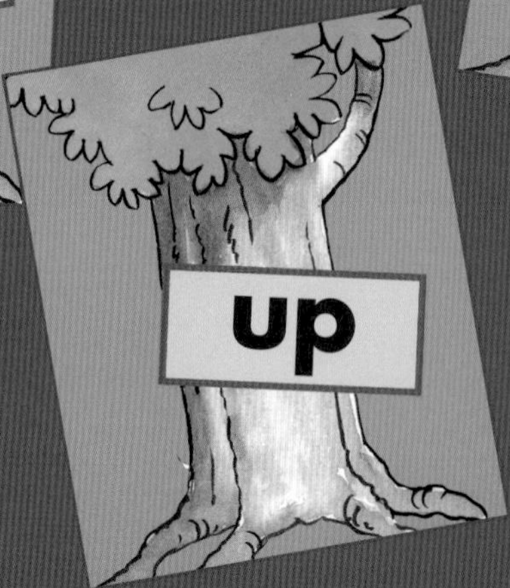
up